The Witch of Hissing Hill

story by Mary Calhoun   pictures by Janet McCaffery

William Morrow & Company New York 1964

Far back in the hill country
is Hissing Hill.
It's a bare lonely spot,
with one twisted house
and a tall fir tree behind it.

And once upon a time
the hill was aswarm
with black witch cats.
Cats arching their backs on the rooftop,
cats chasing up the fir tree,
cats yowling on crooked fence posts,
cats hissing in every corner
of the shackly house.
And all of them black, black, black.
For there lived
a wicked old witch named Sizzle.
She had strings of black hair
and long skinny feet,
and she could figure up more meanness
than any witch in the hills.

But meanness wasn't her main business.
Sizzle raised witch cats.
That was her fame.

Witches came from miles around
to buy their cats from Sizzle.
Her cats were the witchiest,
the wickedest, the very worst,
wonderful witch cats in the world.
Their hisses were jagged
with sharp white teeth.
Their howls made the blood shiver.
Their eyes gleamed yellow with hate.
And definitely, most surely,
Sizzle's cats were the blackest
of all witch cats.
Blacker than Halloween midnight,
they were,
blacker than chimney soot,
blacker than the bottom
of Sizzle's cook pot.
Best, they knew all the wicked ways
of witch cats.
Sizzle taught them.

She taught them spitting and scratching
and scary black slinking.
She taught them
to cross people's paths for bad luck,
and she taught them to yowl.
Most important of all
she taught the cats
staring.
Steady long staring
out of unblinking eyes.
Each cat sat on the witch's hearth,
watching her pot of magic brew.
For when a witch mixes magic,
she needs a black cat to stare at the pot.

It's the look from the cat's eyes
that makes magic work,
that makes a spell jell.
So Sizzle's cats flourished
on Hissing Hill.
Then came Gold.
When Gold was born,
her black mother backed off
and hissed in horror at the sight.

Her only child was yellow, not black.
Oh, the shame of it all!
At first she hid the fluff of yellow
so that Sizzle wouldn't know.
But that was a mistake,
for now Gold had a chance to grow.
Came the day when Sizzle
spied the yellow kitten
bouncing out from under the bed.
Then, oh, the screaming and the scolding!
The old witch was so mad
that her screeches lifted her
two feet off the floor.
Gold's mother was so ashamed
that she lashed her tail
around herself three times
and just purely disappeared.

Gold only purred
and wove her yellow-striped tail
around the witch's bony ankles.
Sizzle's shrieks were so horrible
she sailed right up to the ceiling
and whacked her head.
"Terrible!" she wailed.
"The cat's *nice*!"
Old Sizzle tore at her strings of hair.
What if this yellow female
grew up and had kittens?
She'd ruin the stock!
Whoever heard of
a yellow-striped black witch cat
who was half nice?
What self-respecting witch
would buy her cats?
By witchery, Gold must go!

Sizzle plopped down to the floor.
Grabbing her broom,
she shoved Gold toward the door.
"Out! Out of my house!" she cried.
Now Gold was yellow, and Gold was nice,
but she had a bit of mustard
in her yellow for spice.
She skipped away from the broom,
and with a flicker of her tail
she tickled Sizzle's feet.

"Heh heh heh, oh ha ha!"
cackled the old witch,
hopping up and down
to get away from the tickling.
She swatted at Gold with her broom.
Gold just winked one eye
and flipped her tail.
And the broom straws
turned to yellow-striped feathers.
Shriek! Scream! Howl!

Sizzle's very best magical broom!
She would have killed Gold right there
if she could.
But everyone knows you can't kill a witch cat.
Witch cats only get old and disappear.
Gold sniffed at Sizzle's toes
and slid her tail over them.

Sizzle's feet always hurt,
but Gold's soothing tail
was making the ache go away.
Sizzle almost purred with delight—then—
"Oh no!" she cried.
"Don't come smoothing up to me,
you nasty yellow cat!"

Just then
there was a rushing sound in the sky.
Over the fir tree
flew two witches on their brooms.
"Misery!" cried Sizzle.
"They'll see this yellow cat!
They'll never trust my stock
of black witch cats!"
Pinching up some magic salt,
she sprinkled it on Gold.
"Heckata beckata," she mumbled,
chanting a hasty spell.
And Gold turned into a small yellow pillow.
Sizzle tossed it on her cot
and hurried outside.

Crackle, whump!
Old Witch Hagglestone
landed in Sizzle's herb patch,
crushing the bushes.
Witch Hagglestone was a big bossy witch,
who didn't care what trouble she caused.
Witch Flummery wavered down on her broom,
making a bumpy landing.
"Came to pick a new cat,"
said Old Witch Hagglestone.

She stumped about the yard,
looking for one to suit her.
Witch Flummery fluttered after her.
A snarl of cats
were quarreling under the fir tree,
and Witch Hagglestone picked the winner.
He was a tough tom with fight-notched ears
named Old Scratch.
On a fence post Witch Flummery found
a slant-eyed Jezebel.

Now would they take their cats and go?
Not go near that yellow pillow at all?
No, the visiting witches wanted to test
their cats' powers at staring.
Witch Hagglestone ordered,
"Mix up some magic.
Let's see how these cats work."
She started for the house,
but Sizzle rushed ahead of her.
Good.
Gold was still a pillow on the cot.
So Sizzle threw
herbs and lizard skins into her pot,
and mixed up a brew of hate medicine.

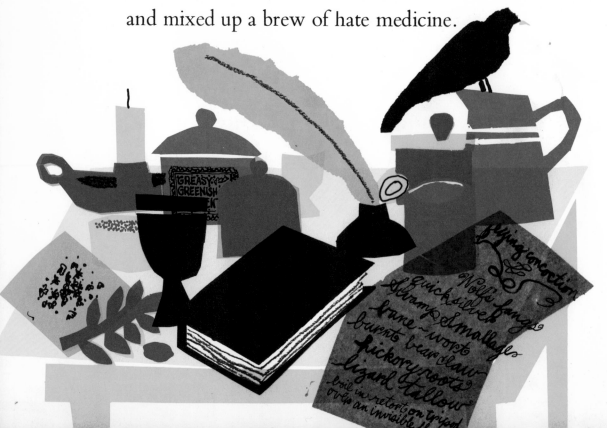

Flummery flopped down on the cot,
and the pillow meowed.
"Oh dear," Flummery cried, peering about.
"Did I sit on a cat?"
"Misery, misery!" whispered Sizzle.
For the yellow pillow was putting out a tail.
Sizzle threw the pillow under the cot
before nearsighted Flummery could see it.
Now the pot of hate medicine
was bubbling angrily.
Witch Sizzle set Old Scratch on the hearth

to do his staring job.

The magical stew sucked and it seethed.

Old Scratch stared at it from the hearth.

And under the cot,

the pillow now had two yellow eyes.

They, too, stared at the pot.

At last the brew gave a loud pop,

and a horrid green steam went up

to signal it was done.

"Fine," said Witch Hagglestone.

"I'll take Old Scratch.

Now let's try out Flummery's cat."
"How is she on spells?"
asked the fluttery witch.
Sizzle felt better
now the hate medicine was done
and Old Hagglestone was satisfied.
"Spells are that cat's specialty," she bragged.
"We'll just turn day into night."
The visiting witches drew in their breaths,
for that was the hardest spell of all.
Jezebel sat in front of Sizzle,
staring with eyes like yellow moons.
The witch whirled around,
wove her arms into twists,
and began to murmur the spell.
As she shrieked the last word
she pointed a bony finger
at the sun through the window. And pop!
Jezebel turned into a yellow cat.
So did Old Scratch.

The sun kept shining, same as ever.
Hagglestone screamed,
and Flummery hid her face in her cloak.
"Yellow!" screeched Old Hagglestone.
"You fool! You've made yellow witch cats!
Don't you know
yellow witch cats are good witch cats?"
Gabbling chants to ward off the goodness,
the two witches
whooshed away on their brooms.
Sizzle stood horrified,
looking at the two yellow cats on her hearth.
Of course!
Yellow witch cats are good witch cats,
full of powerful good magic.
Then Gold, all yellow cat again,
came purring out from under the cot
and wove her tail around the witch's feet.
What a nice little cat she was,
soothing away the ache—no!

Sizzle stopped herself.
Nasty little *good* cat!
Worrisome troublemaker!
She tried to kick Gold.
But somehow her foot wouldn't do it.
By witchery,
the cat's goodness was rubbing off!
Quickly Sizzle drank
a whole cupful of hate medicine.
But sure and true,
Gold was a good witch cat,
and good yellow magic
is stronger than bad black magic.
The stare from her eyes
had changed the brew in the pot.
It wasn't hate medicine at all.
It was love medicine.

Sizzle felt a smile plump out her face,
her bony-claw fingers
smoothed into softness,
and she reached down
to stroke Gold's back.
The wicked old witch
had turned into a loving good witch.
Then Sizzle brought in all of her black cats.
She made a spell with Gold's help,
and pop pop *pop* POP,
every witch cat turned yellow and good.
The cats purred and they played,
and they chased their tails.
And all had mustard
in their yellow for spice.
The winks in their eyes
meant magic for fun.

Sizzle still raises witch cats,
yellow witch cats tricking and tumbling
on Hissing Hill.
Now good witches and fairy godmothers
come from miles around to buy her cats.
For Sizzle's good cats are her fame.
But if you ever see a yellow cat
purring and winking a gold eye, watch out!
For you never know
what a yellow witch cat will do.